Kipper
Story Collection

KIPPER

KIPPER'S TOYBOX

KIPPER'S BIRTHDAY

KIPPER'S SNOWY DAY

*Hodder
Children's
Books*

A division of Hachette Children's Books

This Book
Belongs To:

Kipper

Mick Inkpen

Kipper was in the mood for tidying his basket.

'You are falling apart!' he said to his rabbit.

'You are chewed and you are soggy!' he said to his ball and his bone.

'And you are DISGUSTING!' he said to his smelly old blanket.

Out they went.
'That's better!' said K

But it was not better. Now his basket was uncomfortable.

He twisted and he turned. He wiggled and he wriggled. But it was no good. He could not get comfortable.

'Silly basket!' said Kipper…

…and went outside.

Outside there were two ducks.
They looked very comfortable
standing on one leg.

'That's what I should do!' said
Kipper. But he wasn't very good.
He could only…

...wobble.

Some wrens had made a nest inside
a flowerpot. It looked very cosy.
 'I should sleep in one of those!'
said Kipper. But Kipper would not fit
inside a flowerpot.

He was much too big!

The squirrels had made their nest
out of sticks.

'I will build myself a stick nest!'
said Kipper. But Kipper's nest was
not very good. He could only find…

...three sticks!

The sheep looked very happy
just sitting in the grass.
No, that was no good either.
The grass was much too…

...tickly!

The frog had found a sunny place
in the middle of the pond.
He was sitting on a lily pad.
    'I wonder if I could do that,'
said Kipper.

But he couldn't!

'Perhaps a nice dark hole
would be good,' thought Kipper.
'The rabbits seem to like them.'

But it was not a rabbit hole!

Kipper rushed indoors and hid underneath his blanket.

His

    lovely

        old

            smelly

                blanket!

Kipper put the blanket back in
his basket. He found his rabbit.
   'Sorry, Rabbit,' he said.
He found his bone and his ball.
   'I like my basket just the way it is,'
yawned Kipper. He climbed in and
pulled the blanket over his head.
   'It is the best basket in
the whole, wide…

...sssssssssssshh

hhhhhhh!

Kipper's Toybox

Mick Inkpen

Someone or something had been nibbling a hole in Kipper's toybox.

'I hope my toys are safe,' said Kipper. He emptied them out and counted them.

'One, two, three, four, five, six, SEVEN! That's wrong!' he said. 'There should only be six!'

Kipper counted his toys again.
This time he lined them up to
make it easier.

'Big Owl one, Hippopotamus two,
Sock Thing three, Slipper four,
Rabbit five, Mr Snake six.

That's better!' he said.

Kipper put his toys back in
the toybox. Then he counted them
one more time. Just to make sure.
'One, two, three, four, five,
six, seven, EIGHT NOSES! That's
two too many noses!' said Kipper.

Kipper grabbed Big Owl and
threw him out of the toybox.
'ONE!' he said crossly.
Out went Hippopotamus, 'TWO!'
Out went Rabbit, 'THREE!'
Out went Mr Snake, 'FOUR!'
Out went Slipper, 'FIVE!'
But where was six? Where was
Sock Thing?

Kipper was upset. Next to Rabbit, Sock Thing was his favourite. Now he was gone.

'I won't lose any more of you,' said Kipper. He picked up the rest of his toys and put them in his basket. Then he climbed in and kept watch until bedtime.

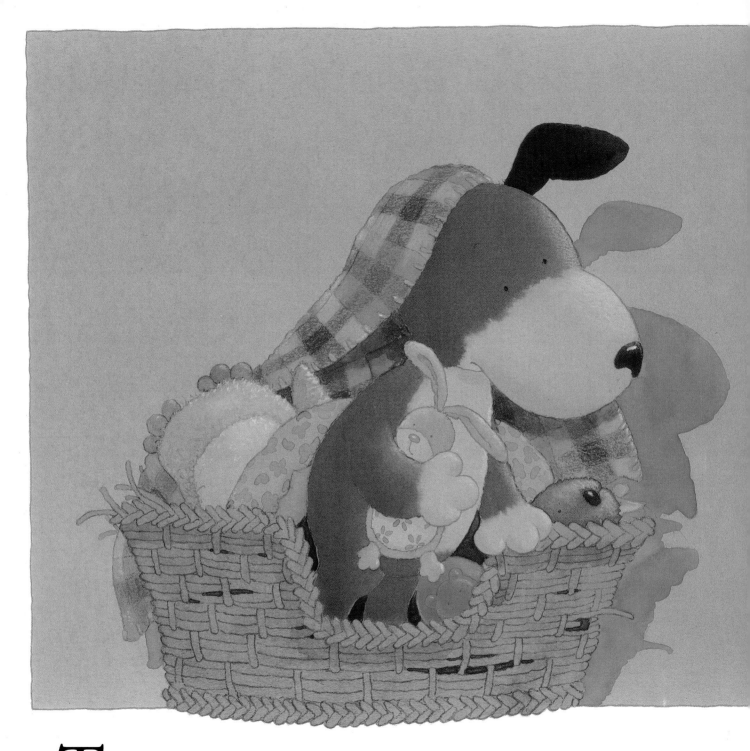

That night Kipper was woken by a strange noise.

It was coming from the corner of the room.

Kipper turned on the light.
There, wriggling across the floor,
was Sock Thing! It must have
been Sock Thing who had been
eating his toybox!

Kipper was not sure what to do.
None of his toys had ever come to
life before. He jumped back in his
basket and hid behind Big Owl.

Sock Thing wriggled slowly round in a circle and bumped into the basket. Then he began to wriggle back the way he had come.

He did not seem to know where he was going. Kipper followed.

Quickly Kipper grabbed him
by the nose. Sock Thing squeaked
and wriggled harder.

Then a little tail appeared.
A little pink tail.

And a little voice said,
'Don't hurt him!'

'So it was YOU! You have been making the hole in my toybox!' said Kipper.

It was true. The mice had been nibbling pieces of Kipper's toybox to make their nest.

'You must promise not to nibble it again,' said Kipper.

'We promise,' said the mice.

In return Kipper let the mice share his basket. It was much cosier than a nest made of cardboard and the two little mice never nibbled Kipper's toybox again…

But their babies did.
They nibbled EVERYTHING!

Kipper's Birthday

Mick Inkpen

It was the day before Kipper's
birthday. He was busy with his
paints making party invitations.
In large letters he painted,

Plees come to my bithday party
tomoro at 12 o cloc dont be lat

He hung them up to dry and set
about making a cake.

Kipper had not made a cake before. He put some currants and eggs and currants and flour and sugar and currants into a bowl. Then he stirred the mixture until his arm ached.

Next he added some cherries and stirred it once more. Then he rolled it with a rolling pin and looked at what he had made.

'I have made a flat thing,' he said.

Kipper squeezed the flat thing into
a cake shape and watched it bake in the
oven. To his surprise it changed itself
slowly into a sort of heap, but it
smelled good. He put the last remaining
cherry on the top for decoration.

By this time the party invitations
were dry.

'I'll deliver them tomorrow,' yawned
Kipper. 'It's too late now.'

Kipper woke bright and early on his birthday. His first thought was, 'Balloons! We must have balloons!' But as he rushed downstairs another thought popped into his head. 'Invitations!'

Kipper ran all the way to his best friend's house and stuffed the invitations into Tiger's hand.

'That one's yours! Those are for the others!' he panted. 'Can't stop! Balloons!'

When he had gone Tiger opened the invitation.

Plees come to my bithday party tomoro at 12 o cloc dont be lat

At twelve o'clock Kipper carefully placed
his cake on the table and sat down to wait
for a knock at the door.

He waited. And he waited. But nobody
came. Not even Tiger.

The cake smelled good and Kipper
began to feel hungry. At one o'clock he
ate the cherry from the top.

Two o'clock passed. Still nobody came. Kipper pulled off a large piece of cake and broke it open to see if there was a cherry inside. There were two. He ate them both and began to feel better.

By five o'clock there were no more cherries to be found.

Kipper stretched out on the table feeling very full and very sleepy.

Kipper slept through the evening and into the night.

He dreamt that he was climbing a mountain made of cake and dodging great cake boulders as they crashed towards him.

Even when the sun streamed through his window the next morning he did not wake, but snored peacefully until noon when he was woken by a knock at the door.

His friends had come.

'Happy birthday, Kipper!' said Jake.

'Happy birthday, Kipper!' said Holly.

'And many happy returns!' said Tiger. Kipper blinked and rubbed his eyes.

'But my birthday was yesterday,' he said sleepily.

They looked at the invitation.

Plees come to my bithday party tomoro at 12 o cloc dont be lat

Kipper looked puzzled.
'So my birthday is not until tomorrow,' he said. 'We haven't missed it after all!'

'No, no, no,' said Tiger. 'Your birthday must have been *tomorrow* the day before yesterday.' Kipper looked puzzled again.

Tiger went on, 'So yesterday it would have been *today,* but today it was *yesterday.* Do you see?'

Kipper did not see. His brain was beginning to ache so he said, 'Cake anyone?' And then he remembered that he had eaten it all.

'Never mind,' said Tiger. 'Why don't you open your presents?'

The presents seemed a bit odd.
The first was a napkin from Jake.
The second was some candles from Holly.

'Very useful,' said Kipper, trying not to look disappointed.

But the third was the most useful of all…

It was a cake!

Kipper's Snowy Day

Mick Inkpen

It was a new morning
and it was snowing!
Huge cotton wool snowflakes were
tumbling past Kipper's window.

'Yes!' said Kipper, jumping out
of his basket. 'Yes! Yes!'

He grabbed his scarf and wound
it three times round his head.
'Yes! Yes! Yes!'

Kipper was very positive
about snow.

Kipper rushed outside. The snow lay deep and smooth and new, like an empty page waiting to be scribbled on. He made a paw print, and then another.

And then with a whoop he went charging round and round, criss-crossing this way and that, until the garden was full of his tracks.

Kipper stopped to catch his breath, letting the swirling snowflakes melt on his tongue. Then he fell backwards into the snow and lay there panting.

When he stood up he found that he had made a perfect Kipper shaped hole. He tried again. Then he tried a different shape. And another.

'I bet Tiger hasn't thought of this,' he said, and ran off to find his best friend.

Kipper found Tiger at the top of Big Hill. He was wrapped up in a fat bundle of silly, woolly clothes. Kipper plopped a friendly snowball on top of his head.

'Hello,' said Tiger.

Tiger pointed up at the sky. A watery sun was seeping through the grey clouds.

'It won't last,' he said. 'It'll all be gone by tomorrow. There's a warm wind coming.' Tiger was like that. He knew things.

But this was not at all what
Kipper wanted to hear, so he started
throwing snowballs at his friend.

Tiger was very easy to hit
because the silly, woolly clothes were
wrapped so tightly around him that
he could hardly move.
And his own snowballs
stuck like little pompoms
to the silly, woolly
gloves.

'Look at my new
game,' said Kipper,
falling backwards into
the snow.
'You get up very carefully…
and there you are!' And there he was,
or at least the shape of him.
Tiger stretched out his arms, and
fell backwards with a soft, woolly
'crump'. But when he tried to get up
he could not. He was too round.
He just lay there waving his arms
and legs like a beetle on its back.

Tiger heaved himself over onto his tummy, but rolled too far, and found himself on his back again. He tried again. The same thing happened. Snow began to stick in thick lumps to the silly, woolly clothes. Crossly, he heaved himself over once more.

This time he rolled over twice, three times, four times...

Slowly at first,
and then a little faster,
and then a lot faster,
and then very fast indeed,
he rolled down the hill.

And as he went the silly, woolly
clothes picked up more and more
snow, so that by the time he
reached the bottom he had changed
from a small dog into a giant
snowball. The giant snowball
fell to pieces.

Kipper charged down the hill.
'Are you all right, Tiger?' he panted.
Tiger pulled off his silly, woolly hat.
A big grin spread across his face.
'Again!' he said.

So that is what they did, all
day long, taking turns to wear the
silly, woolly clothes.

And by the time the sun began
to dip towards the hill, making their
shadows long and skinny, they had
rolled enough snow to the bottom to
build a giant snowdog.

They watched their shadows
lengthen and fade.

'It'll all be gone by tomorrow,'
said Tiger. 'There's a warm
wind coming.'

But for once
Tiger was wrong.
The warm wind stayed
away, and that night
another snowstorm smoothed out all
of Kipper's paw prints, making the
garden like a clean, white, empty
page once more.

And the snowdog stood at the
bottom of Big Hill wearing Tiger's
silly, woolly clothes...

For almost three . . .   whole . . .

weeks.

This collection first published in 1998
by Hodder Children's Books

Kipper first published 1991
Kipper's Toybox first published 1992
Kipper's Birthday first published 1993
Kipper's Snowy Day first published 1996

Text and illustrations copyright © Mick Inkpen 1991, 1992, 1993, 1996

Hodder Children's Books
338 Euston Road
London NW1 3BH

Hodder Children's Books Australia
Level 17/207 Kent Street
Sydney, NSW 2000

The right of Mick Inkpen to be identified as the author
of this work has been asserted by him in accordance with
the Copyright, Designs and Patents Act 1988.

A catalogue record of this book is available from the British Library.

ISBN: 978 0 340 74676 9
23 24 25 26 27 28 29 30

Printed in China

Hodder Children's Books is a division of Hachette Children's Books
An Hachette UK Company
www.hachette.co.uk

Goodbye.